BIBLE WORD SEARCH

Songs of Grace and Glory

No part of this book may be scanned, reproduced or distributed in any printed or electronic form without the prior permission of the author or publisher.

COPYRIGHT 2024 - HealyPanda Publishing

Christian Hymns

1. *Amazing Grace*
2. *How Great Thou Art*
3. *Great Is Thy Faithfulness*
4. *Holy, Holy, Holy*
5. *Be Thou My Vision*
6. *It Is Well with My Soul*
7. *Blessed Assurance*
8. *The Old Rugged Cross*
9. *A Mighty Fortress Is Our God*
10. *Come Thou Fount of Every Blessing*
11. *What a Friend We Have in Jesus*
12. *Jesus Paid It All*
13. *To God Be the Glory*
14. *Rock of Ages*
15. *Just As I Am*
16. *Crown Him with Many Crowns*
17. *All Hail the Power of Jesus' Name*
18. *Fairest Lord Jesus*
19. *I Surrender All*
20. *O for a Thousand Tongues to Sing*
21. *Joyful, Joyful, We Adore Thee*
22. *I Need Thee Every Hour*

# of Grace and Glory

Amazing Grace

Amazing grace! How **sweet** the **sound**
That saved a wretch like me!
I once was lost, but now am **found**,
Was **blind**, but now I see.

'Twas grace that taught my **heart** to **fear**,
And **grace** my fears **relieved**;
How **precious** did that grace **appear**
The **hour** I first **believed**.

Through many **dangers**, toils, and **snares**,
I have already **come**;
'Tis grace hath brought me **safe** thus far,
And grace will lead me **home**.

The **Lord** has **promised good** to me,
His word my **hope secures**;
He will my **shield** and portion be,
As long as life **endures**.

How Great Thou Art

O Lord my God, When I, in **awesome wonder**,
Consider all the **worlds** Thy Hands have made;
I see the **stars**, I hear the rolling **thunder**,
Thy **power** throughout the **universe** displayed.

Then **sings** my soul, My **Saviour** God, to Thee,
How **great** Thou art, How great Thou art.
Then sings my **soul**, My Saviour God, to Thee,
How great Thou art, How great Thou art!

When through the **woods** and **forest glades** I **wander**,
And hear the **birds** sing **sweetly** in the trees.
When I look down, from lofty mountain grandeur
And see the **brook**, and feel the **gentle breeze**.

And when I think, that God, His Son not sparing;
Sent Him to die, I **scarce** can take it in;
That on a **Cross**, my **burdens** gladly bearing,
He **bled** and died to take away my sin.

Great Is Thy Faithfulness

Great is Thy faithfulness, O God my **Father**;
there is no **shadow** of **turning** with Thee;
Thou **changest** not, Thy **compassions**, they fail not;
as Thou hast been, Thou **forever** wilt be.

Great is Thy **faithfulness**!
Great is Thy faithfulness!
Morning by **morning** new mercies I see;
all I have needed Thy **hand** hath **provided**:
great is Thy faithfulness, Lord, unto me!

Summer and **winter**, and **springtime** and **harvest**;
sun, **moon**, and **stars** in their **courses** **above**
join with all **nature** in **manifold** **witness**
to Thy great faithfulness, **mercy**, and **love**.

Pardon for sin and a **peace** that endureth,
Thine own dear **presence** to cheer and to **guide**;
strength for today and bright hope for tomorrow:
blessings all mine, with ten **thousand** beside!

```
C M O O N N P N S U M M E R O
U W I N T E R E S T A R S V K
W R X P V H V F A S Z X T F T
B U X O A W U X U C Z S I Q Y
E F L G P R O V I D E D J O O
F W A F N H D H O G L Y J C L
T T C I A I E O N S C I E O Z
N Y V N T A N A N R H V M M R
W A D W L H H R E L O T I P P
W O T E A C F M U B C B T A S
N K D U P V M U A T A V G S T
P E M A R S O D L F I G N S R
Z C A V H E R N S N W G I I E
R N N Q Y S N A I S E A R O N
E E I Z U R I S T A E S P N G
V S F N G U N U T J O N S S T
E E O Y X O G O E O D D T S H
R R L O E C B H E D I U G I K
O P D U R F T T S E V R A H W
F S P C F A T H E R R J I V I
```

Holy, Holy, Holy

Holy, **holy**, holy! Lord God **Almighty**!
Early in the **morning** our **song** shall rise to Thee;
Holy, holy, holy! **merciful** and mighty!
God in three **Persons**, blessed **Trinity**!

Holy, holy, holy! all the **saints adore** Thee,
casting down their **golden crowns** around the
glassy sea;
cherubim and seraphim, falling down before Thee,
which wert and art and **evermore** shalt be.

Holy, holy, holy! though the **darkness** hide Thee,
though the eye of **sinful** man Thy glory may not see;
only Thou art holy, there is none **beside** Thee,
perfect in pow'r, in **love**, and **purity**.

Holy, holy, holy! Lord God Almighty!
All Thy **works** shall **praise** Thy name, in **earth** and
sky and sea;
Holy, holy, holy! merciful and **mighty**!
God in three Persons, **blessed** Trinity!

Be Thou My Vision

Be Thou my **Vision**, O Lord of my **heart**;
Naught be all else to me, save that Thou art.
Thou my best **Thought**, by day or by **night**,
Waking or **sleeping**, Thy **presence** my light.

Be Thou my **Wisdom**, and Thou my true **Word**;
I ever with Thee and Thou with me, Lord;
Thou my great Father, I Thy true son;
Thou in me **dwelling**, and I with Thee one.

Be Thou my **battle Shield**, **Sword** for the fight;
Be Thou my **Dignity**, Thou my **Delight**;
Thou my soul's **Shelter**, Thou my high **Tower**:
Raise Thou me **heavenward**, O Power of my
power.

Riches I heed not, nor man's empty **praise**,
Thou mine **Inheritance**, now and always:
Thou and Thou only, **first** in my heart,
High King of **Heaven**, my **Treasure** Thou art.

It Is Well with My Soul

When **peace**, like a **river**, **attendeth** my way,
When **sorrows** like sea **billows** roll;
Whatever my lot, Thou hast **taught** me to say,
It is well, it is **well** with my soul.

It is well with my **soul**,
It is well, it is well with my soul.

Though Satan should **buffet**, though **trials** should
come,
Let this **blest** assurance **control**,
That **Christ** hath regarded my **helpless** estate,
And hath shed His own **blood** for my soul.

My sin—oh, the **bliss** of this **glorious** thought!—
My sin, not in part but the **whole**,
Is **nailed** to the **cross**, and I bear it no more,
Praise the Lord, praise the Lord, O my soul!

And Lord, haste the day when the **faith** shall be **sight**,
The **clouds** be rolled **back** as a **scroll**;
The trump shall **resound**, and the Lord shall **descend**,
Even so, it is well with my soul.

Blessed Assurance

Blessed **assurance**, Jesus is mine
Oh, what a **foretaste** of **glory** **divine**
Heir of **salvation**, **purchase** of God
Born of his **Spirit**, washed in His **blood**.

This is my **story**, this is my song
Praising my Savior all the day long
This is my story, this is my song
Praising my **Savior** all the day long.

Perfect **submission**, perfect **delight**
Visions of **rapture** now burst on my **sight**
Angels **descending** bring from above
Echoes of **mercy**, **whispers** of **love**.

This is my story, this is my **song**
Praising my Savior all the day **long**
This is my story, this is my song
Praising my Savior all the day long
Praising my Savior all the day long

The Old Rugged Cross

On a **hill** far away stood an old **rugged** cross,
the **emblem** of **suffering** and **shame**;
and I love that old cross where the **dearest** and best
for a world of lost **sinners** was **slain**.

So I'll **cherish** the old rugged **cross**,
till my **trophies** at last I lay down;
I will cling to the old rugged cross,
and **exchange** it some day for a **crown**.

O that old rugged cross, so **despised** by the **world**,
has a **wondrous attraction** for me;
for the dear **Lamb** of God left his **glory** above
to bear it to **dark Calvary**.

In that old rugged cross, **stained** with **blood** so **divine**,
a wondrous **beauty** I see,
for 'twas on that old cross Jesus **suffered** and died,
to **pardon** and **sanctify** me.

A Mighty Fortress

A **mighty** **fortress** is our God,
A **bulwark** never **failing**;
Our **helper** He, amid the **flood**
Of **mortal** ills **prevailing**:
For still our **ancient** foe
Doth seek to work us woe;
His **craft** and **power** are great,
And, **armed** with **cruel hate**,
On **earth** is not his **equal**.

Did we in our own **strength confide**,
Our **striving** would be **losing**;
Were not the right Man on our side,
The Man of God's own **choosing**:
Dost ask who that may be?
Christ Jesus, it is He;
Lord **Sabaoth**, His name,
From age to age the same,
And He must win the **battle**.

```
B B D B K M H L O S I N G J P
A U I D O M P S F L F I E Z R
V L O R O E T A H R R X K G E
U W T C X E G S J X F G W S V
F A Y K L Y S V F L O O D U A
L R O T M E J L T D F P S L I
A K T H R T E P E S E C P P L
G A C T H E S Q P U Q M R A I
B U R R H Q U I C V R H R G N
W O F A P U S Y R O W C B A G
F U M E H A A L O H N H W G B
P T U B E L C S X M C F N A G
Z N F P L X H P T F I I I N V
B E B S P W H T U R S G I D J
X I T C E S I L O O E L H P E
N C P I R N N C O A I N L T C
V N O C X G M H R A B S G X Y
F A W U D N C E F A T A C T K
V Z E Y I I P Z F F F Z S V H
R E R S T R I V I N G T D A X
```

Come Thou Fount

Come Thou **fount** of every **blessing**
Tune my **heart** to sing Thy **grace**
Streams of **mercy** never **ceasing**
Call for **songs** of **loudest** praise.

Teach me some **melodious sonnet**
Sung by **flaming tongues** above
Praise the **mount**, I'm fixed upon it
Mount of Thy **redeeming** love.

Here I raise my **Ebenezer**
Here by Thy great **help** I've come
And I hope by Thy good **pleasure**
Safely to **arrive** at home.

Jesus sought me when a **stranger**
Wandering from the fold of God
He to **rescue** me from **danger**
Interposed His **precious blood**.

What a Friend We Have

What a friend we have in **Jesus**,
all our **sins** and **griefs** to bear!
What a **privilege** to carry
everything to God in prayer!
O what **peace** we often **forfeit**,
O what **needless** pain we **bear**,
all **because** we do not **carry**
everything to God in prayer!

Have we **trials** and **temptations**?
Is there **trouble anywhere**?
We **should** never be **discouraged**;
take it to the Lord in **prayer**!
Can we find a **friend** so **faithful**
who will all our **sorrows** share?
Jesus knows our every **weakness**;
take it to the **Lord** in prayer!

Jesus Paid It All

I hear the **Savior** say,
"Thy **strength** indeed is **small**,
Child of **weakness**, **watch** and pray,
Find in Me thine all in all."

Jesus paid it all,
All to Him I owe;
Sin had left a **crimson stain**,
He **washed** it white as **snow**.

Lord, now indeed I find
Thy pow'r and Thine **alone**,
Can **change** the leper's **spots**
And melt the **heart** of **stone**.

For **nothing good** have I
Where-by Thy **grace** to **claim**;
I'll wash my **garments white**
In the **blood** of Calv'ry's **Lamb**.

To God Be the Glory

To God be the **glory**, great things he has **done**!
So **loved** he the **world** that he gave us his
Son,
who **yielded** his **life** an **atonement** for sin,
and **opened** the life-gate that all may go in.

Praise the Lord! Praise the **Lord**,
Let the **earth** hear his **voice**!
Praise the Lord! Praise the Lord!
Let the **people rejoice**!
O come to the **Father** through **Jesus** the Son
and give him the glory, great **things** he has
done!

Great things he has **taught** us, great things he
has done,
and great our rejoicing through Jesus the Son,
but **purer** and **higher** and **greater** will be
our joy and our **wonder**, when Jesus we see.

Page 28

```
O A R O J D E E L D E V O L C
K T O M X N R O R K Y K L L I
L O P P O I R E T H J E H Y U
U N E D I Z R X N I Y W J I C
E E N Z Y U P R A I S E K T V
X M E W P G T W O R L D Y F W
H E D F E E C D N J F Q Y E W
R N H T C E J C E M X B O O I
H T B I Z B T S P D R N N D O
P Z O Y J A U S H E L D G Y R
E V E D U S W I H T E E R T D
O X V G E V K G P R H O I B O
P I H J I M I D J V L I J Y H
L T K E K H A G E G L K N I L
E I N O A L W L C V S O C G D
H V F F I R O I I S N D R W S
U T M E H Q T L O E O O U D U
R E T A E R G H J G T Q Q M V
R G Q Y P I O X E C H N I I R
F A T H E R A W R M M Q A M G
```

Rock of Ages

Rock of **Ages**, cleft for me,
Let me **hide** myself in Thee;
Let the **water** and the **blood**,
From Thy **riven** side which **flowed**,
Be of sin the **double cure**,
Save me from its **guilt** and **power**.

Not the **labor** of my **hands**
Can fulfill Thy law's **demands**;
Could my zeal no respite know,
Could my **tears** forever flow,
All could never sin **erase**,
Thou must save, and save by **grace**.

Nothing in my hands I **bring**,
Simply to Thy **cross** I **cling**;
Naked, come to Thee for **dress**,
Helpless, look to Thee for grace:
Foul, I to the **fountain** fly,
Wash me, Savior, or I die.

Just As I Am

Just as I am, **without** one plea,
But that Thy **blood** was shed for me,
And that Thou **bidst** me come to Thee,
O **Lamb** of God, I come, I come.

Just as I am, and **waiting** not
To rid my **soul** of one **dark blot**,
To Thee whose blood can **cleanse** each **spot**,
O Lamb of God, I come, I **come**.

Just as I am, though **tossed** about
With many a **conflict**, many a **doubt**,
Fightings and **fears within**, without,
O Lamb of God, I come, I come.

Just as I am, **poor**, **wretched**, **blind**;
Sight, **riches**, **healing** of the **mind**,
Yea, all I need in Thee to **find**,
O Lamb of God, I come, I come.

Crown Him with Many Crowns

Crown Him with many crowns,
The **Lamb** upon His **throne**;
Hark! How the heav'nly **anthem drowns**
All **music** but its own!
Awake, my **soul** and **sing**
Of Him Who **died** for **thee**,
And hail Him as thy **matchless King**
Through all **eternity**.

Crown Him the Lord of love!
Behold His hands and side—
Rich wounds, yet **visible above**,
In **beauty glorified**.
No **angel** in the sky
Can fully **bear** that **sight**,
But **downward** bends His wond'ring eye
At **mysteries** so **bright**.

```
M T A A M Q G L O R I F I E D
M W E W U B A N S Y M E E H T
I T Q N S Z M I C A J U V Y V
M K K M I T G A T R X S U V I
Y Y I W C H K C L V O I E X S
O B S Q T I H A L U X W C U I
E T B T P L W E L A V H N B B
K H D O E A N T H E M E D E L
Z R L S K R U H W X L B N H E
J O S E X U I J E E T Z J O E
R N C D B F E E G S H I M L D
M E A B O V E N S N G U R D B
G A A X T P A S M K I D W P O
M S A D Y M D P R N R R D L U
Y I R T P R I X D Z B A H I O
T N Q H E Z E R G R G W G T V
U G Q U T M D W I D O N S Y D
A R W O U N D S F C I W Z P L
E Y T I N R E T E K H O N E Z
B S O C W J I R A E B D H S Q
```

All Hail the Power of Jesus' Name

All **hail** the **power** of Jesus' **name**!
Let **angels prostrate fall**;
Bring **forth** the **royal** diadem,
And crown Him **Lord** of all.
Bring forth the royal **diadem**,
And **crown** Him Lord of all.

Ye **chosen seed** of Israel's **race**,
Ye **ransomed** from the fall,
Hail Him who saves you by his **grace**,
And crown Him Lord of all.
Hail Him who **saves** you by his grace,
And crown Him Lord of all.

Sinners, whose love can ne'er **forget**
The **wormwood** and the **gall**,
Go **spread** your trophies at His **feet**,
And crown Him Lord of all.
Go spread your **trophies** at His feet,
And crown Him Lord of all.

Fairest Lord Jesus

Fairest Lord Jesus, **Ruler** of all **nature**,
O Thou of God and man the Son,
Thee will I **cherish**, Thee will I **honor**,
Thou, my soul's **glory**, joy and **crown**.

Fair are the **meadows**, fairer still the
woodlands,
Robed in the **blooming** garb of **spring**;
Jesus is fairer, Jesus is **purer**,
Who **makes** the **woeful heart** to **sing**.

All fairest **beauty**, **heavenly** and **earthly**,
Wondrously, Jesus, is found in Thee;
None can be **nearer**, fairer or **dearer**,
Than Thou, my Savior, art to me.

Beautiful **Savior**! Lord of all the **nations**!
Son of God and Son of Man!
Glory and honor, praise, **adoration**,
Now and **forevermore** be **Thine**.

I Surrender All

All to Jesus I **surrender**,
All to Him I **freely give**;
I will ever **love** and **trust** Him,
In His **presence daily live**.

I surrender all, I surrender all;
All to **Thee**, my **blessed Savior**,
I surrender all.

All to **Jesus** I surrender,
Make me, Savior, **wholly** Thine;
Let me feel Thy **Holy Spirit**,
Truly know that Thou art **mine**.

All to Jesus I surrender,
Lord, I give **myself** to Thee;
Fill me with Thy love and **power**,
Let Thy **blessing fall** on me.

```
Z L E D U B T S U R T D G T V
F I N K K K L A F V V X I I Q
H V V J A T B E K X X I V Z Q
F E W X F Y H L S D F N E N C
A Y T Q F B Y E E S S V M G Y
L H L D Q L H H E S I N S O L
L D H I L H O L Y Z S N E W E
K O X O A L O V E Q X E G R E
T T H J Q D S C T F N I D E R
D W R U J M D N L U N C N D F
N U I U B N S E S E A K O N T
A B R C L H S P O M D W E E G
Q R Y Z A Y I U R B I C Q R S
U C Q P M R E R A X N Y S R V
H S F I I W N R S E X A L U U
Z F J T I C I L S A B M O S O
Z A E C Q B M E U M V Y R B X
H I S F H T R N N Y L I D M X
C E U L Y P B I X U V Q O K C
K F S P O W E R W V V A G R G
```

O for a Thousand Tongues

O for a **thousand** **tongues** to **sing**
my great Redeemer's praise,
the glories of my God and **King**,
the **triumphs** of his **grace**!

My **gracious Master** and my God,
assist me to **proclaim**,
to **spread** thro' all the **earth abroad**
the **honors** of your **name**.

Jesus! the name that **charms** our **fears**,
that bids our **sorrows cease**,
'tis **music** in the sinner's ears,
'tis **life** and **health** and **peace**.

He **breaks** the **power** of **cancelled** sin,
he sets the **prisoner free**;
his **blood** can **make** the **foulest clean**;
his blood **availed** for me.

Joyful, Joyful, We Adore Thee

Joyful, joyful, we **adore** Thee,
God of **glory**, Lord of love;
Hearts unfold like flow'rs before Thee,
Op'ning to the sun **above**.
Melt the **clouds** of sin and **sadness**;
Drive the **dark** of **doubt away**;
Giver of **immortal gladness**,
Fill us with the **light** of day!

All Thy **works** with joy **surround** Thee,
Earth and heav'n **reflect** Thy **rays**,
Stars and **angels** sing around Thee,
Center of **unbroken** praise.
Field and **forest**, **vale** and **mountain**,
Flow'ry **meadow**, **flashing** sea,
Singing bird and **flowing fountain**
Call us to **rejoice** in Thee.

I Need Thee Every Hour

I **need** Thee ev'ry **hour**,
Most **gracious** Lord;
No **tender voice** like Thine
Can **peace afford**.

I need Thee, oh, I need **Thee**;
Ev'ry hour I need Thee;
Oh, **bless** me now, my **Savior**,
I **come** to Thee.

I need Thee ev'ry hour,
Stay Thou **nearby**;
Temptations lose their pow'r
When Thou art **nigh**.

I need Thee ev'ry hour,
In joy or **pain**;
Come **quickly** and **abide**,
Or **life** is **vain**.

```
S D Z L L A A U A E E E L W V
W U L W A U A P Q W N J Y W R
D G O B V H V O I C E L Y E X
P U F I H A L X C U K I Q G Z
E D B P C V I H V C E L I E C
G R A I Y A I N I Y P R Q I T
B A D B I R R U K C U S X D T
Q X E T I E Q G L O H I X B V
X H E T G D Q Y H N E A R B Y
T B N J E N E V R Q V S X L E
F E P J F E M G J Y Z A E L B
N Z M E I T J P A I N V L T O
H T H P L U C D M E A I G O L
V G R A T C R K R G Q O M G Y
N R I R X A S Z L O P R E B X
T G D N I U T M C S F E B Z B
X P N C O M E I S U H F M S J
S P E A C E B E O T F F A O X
B N U Y Y A L Q R N E C T U I
N F V I E B P L A I S J Q U L
```

Because He Lives

God sent His son, they **called** Him Jesus;
He came to love, **heal** and **forgive**;
He **lived** and **died** to buy my **pardon**,
An empty **grave** is there to **prove** my **Savior** lives!

Because He lives, I can face **tomorrow**,
Because He lives, all fear is gone;
Because I know He holds the **future**,
And life is **worth** the living,
Just because He lives!

How **sweet** to hold a **newborn** baby,
And feel the **pride** and joy he **gives**;
But greater still the calm **assurance**:
This child can face **uncertain** days because He
Lives!

And then one day, I'll **cross** the **river**,
I'll **fight** life's **final** war with pain;
And then, as **death** gives way to **victory**,
I'll see the **lights** of glory and I'll know He lives!

When I Survey

When I **survey** the **wondrous** cross
On which the **Prince** of Glory died,
My **richest** gain I **count** but loss,
And pour **contempt** on all my **pride**.

Forbid it, Lord, that I should **boast**
Save in the **death** of **Christ**, my God;
All the vain **things** that **charm** me most
I **sacrifice** them to His **blood**.

See, from His **head**, His **hands**, His **feet**,
Sorrow and love flow **mingled down**;
Did e'er such love and sorrow meet,
Or **thorns compose** so rich a **crown**?

Were the whole realm of **nature** mine,
That were a **present** far too small;
Love so **amazing**, so **Divine**,
Demands my soul, my life, my all.

Turn Your Eyes Upon Jesus

O **soul**, are you **weary** and **troubled**?
No **light** in the **darkness** you see?
There's light for a look at the **Savior**,
And life more **abundant** and free!

Turn your eyes upon Jesus,
Look full in His **wonderful face**,
And the things of **earth** will grow **strangely**
dim,
In the light of His **glory** and **grace**.

Thro' **death** into life **everlasting**,
He **passed**, and we **follow** Him there;
O'er us sin no more hath **dominion**--
For more than conqu'rors we are!

His **Word** shall not **fail** you--He **promised**;
Believe Him, and all will be well:
Then go to a **world** that is **dying**,
His **perfect salvation** to tell!

Christ the Lord Is Risen Today

Christ the Lord is ris'n **today**, Alleluia!
Sons of men and **angels** say, Alleluia!
Raise your joys and **triumphs high**, Alleluia!
Sing, ye heav'ns, and **earth**, **reply**, Alleluia!

Lives again our **glorious King**, Alleluia!
Where, O **death**, is now thy **sting**? Alleluia!
Once He **died** our **souls** to **save**, Alleluia!
Where thy **victory**, O **grave**? Alleluia!

Love's **redeeming work** is done, Alleluia!
Fought the **fight**, the **battle** won, Alleluia!
Death in **vain forbids** His rise, Alleluia!
Christ hath **opened paradise**, Alleluia!

Soar we now where Christ hath led, Alleluia!
Foll'wing our **exalted Head**, Alleluia!
Made like Him, like Him we rise, **Alleluia**!
Ours the **cross**, the grave, the **skies**, Alleluia!

```
Z S S O R C T O D A Y F P G H
G T J E A S F O R B I D S E P
A N R E P S O M N G A O X A S
K L I I A P Q U O N V O R Z P
D V L M U R Y T L C V A J B B
P E K E E M T L I S D B D E T
D V A I L E P H P I B E F T O
H L J T N U D H S E I Y I U P
M A A W H G I E S D R W G Z E
C H R I S T P A R O Z Z H C N
A G S T J F A D T S S N T D E
S L K C V D E C E Q A T Q J D
M Y I F Q X I V K H W V I U V
C Z E D A V A B G I Q O E N R
V T S L L R T D X G I C R K G
Y W T S G N V D G H F V U K J
M E S S I U X A N G E L S T B
D C C A O B A T T L E T Q U K
H W V G L O R I O U S F Y S T
V D I H E A D T H G U O F U W
```

He Lives

I **serve** a risen **Saviour**, He's in the world today
I know that He is **living**, whatever men may say
I see His **hand** of **mercy**, I hear His **voice** of
cheer
And just the **time** I need Him He's **always** near.

He lives, He lives, **Christ Jesus** lives **today**
He **walks** with me and **talks** with me
Along life's **narrow** way
He lives, He lives, **Salvation** to **impart**
You ask me how I know He lives?
He lives within my **heart**.

In all the **world around** me I see His loving care
And though my heart grows **weary** I never will
despair
I know that He is **leading**, through all the
stormy blast
The day of His **appearing** will come at last.

I'd Rather Have Jesus

I'd rather have **Jesus** than **silver** or **gold**;
I'd rather be His than have **riches** **untold**;
I'd rather have Jesus than **houses** or **lands**;
I'd rather be led by His nail-pierced **hand**.

Than to be the king of a vast **domain**
Or be held in sin's **dread** sway;
I'd rather have Jesus than **anything**
This **world** **affords** **today**.

I'd rather have Jesus than men's **applause**;
I'd rather be **faithful** to His dear **cause**;
I'd rather have Jesus than **worldwide** **fame**;
I'd rather be true to His holy name.

He's **fairer** than **lilies** of **rarest** **bloom**;
He's **sweeter** than **honey** from out the **comb**;
He's all that my **hungering** **spirit** **needs**;
I'd rather have Jesus and let Him **lead**.

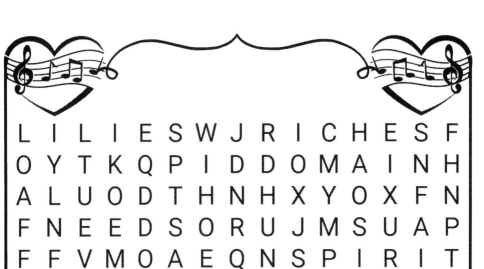

```
L I L I E S W J R I C H E S F
O Y T K Q P I D D O M A I N H
A L U O D T H N H X Y O X F N
F N E E D S O R U J M S U A P
F F V M O A E Q N S P I R I T
O D C Y L T Y Q G O S C C T F
R E R C E L V W E T Y Z X H A
D G H E Z A C G R Q R F R F I
S W W O A N B D I Q F W J U R
M S O K U D P E N L S D F L E
Y J I R U S S Z G N I Y A W R
S D N L L U E T Y J L B M O S
G N O N A D L S D E V A E R K
O A F L D B W L J S E Z Z L H
C H P A L U O I P U R W I D N
R P E O N G L C D S W P D P S
A L O T S E H O N E Y I T T H
F M O N P X E R A R E S T B B
R L A N Y T H I N G W S T L M
D S C A U S E B M O C M W Y G
```

Victory in Jesus

I **heard** an old, old **story** how a **Savior** came from **glory,**
How He gave His **life** on **Calvary** to save a **wretch** like me;
I heard about His **groaning**, of His **precious** blood's **atoning,**
Then I **repented** of my sins and won the **victory.**

O victory in Jesus, my Savior, **forever!**
He **sought** me and **bought** me with His **redeeming blood;**
He loved me ere I knew Him, and all my love is due Him.
He **plunged** me to victory beneath the **cleansing flood.**

I heard about His **healing**, of His cleansing pow'r **revealing**
How he made the lame to walk again and **caused** the **blind** to see;
And then I **cried**, "Dear Jesus, come and heal my **broken spirit**,"
And some **sweet** day I'll sing up there the **song** of victory.

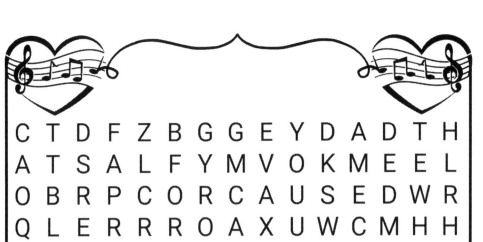

C T D F Z B G G E Y D A D T H
A T S A L F Y M V O K M E E L
O B R P C O R C A U S E D W R
Q L E R R R O A X U W C M H H
N O V E O E L D F S G E S L S
E O E C I V G L B N R Q B P E
K D A I V E U T I E Q Q I H A
O H L O A R H S D T D R C L G
R B I U S G N E H E I T B Y N
B M N S U A E G G T E F T H I
T B G O E M U N C R Q Y U D N
J Y B L I O U U W A L B R X A
X R C N S L X L H B L A P S O
F O G A P M R H E D E V Y S R
A T O N I N G D A H E V A E G
C C O B G N O S L Y F I L R Z
Q I M F L F R V I R A L R W Y
H V W G Q I L P N O V I S C D
S R A Y L A N V G T J F K E L
R E P E N T E D D S R E I R A

Love Lifted Me

I was **sinking** deep in sin, far from the **peaceful shore**,
Very **deeply stained** within, sinking to rise no more,
But the Master of the sea **heard** my **despairing** cry,
From the **waters lifted** me, now **safe** am I.

Love lifted me!
Love lifted me!
When **nothing** else could **help**,
Love lifted me!

All my **heart** to Him I **give**, ever to Him I'll **cling**,
In His **blessed presence** live, ever His **praises** sing,
Love so **mighty** and so true, **merits** my soul's best **songs**,
Faithful, **loving service**, too, to Him **belongs**.

Souls in **danger**, look **above**, Jesus **completely saves**,
He will lift you by His love, out of the **angry waves**;
He's the **Master** of the sea, **billows** His will obey,
He your Savior wants to be, be saved today.

```
E H E A R T G L U H E L P Q C
S E R V I C E N E A Y S F E L
M A S T E R R C I B E G T M I
I H F A O E N D F V U K E L N
B H U E G E S L A E O L C T G
I W J N S R J S I A R L F C N
L G A E P G D L T G L O C O O
L D R Q B G T X H U I O H A T
O P H Q L S A D F D M V N S H
W E E F E X T E U P G G E E I
S A A N S M C A L N R Z A V N
O O R R S A B E I Y W O Z O G
N N D M E A T K L N M B Z B B
G Y U P D E N S S W E X W A L
S R A G L I D H E G A D D L I
O W T Y S K G Q U S N V M B F
D E S P A I R I N G I O E M T
Y U D E E P L Y P N G A L S E
C K S W T S R E T A W W R E D
M E R I T S M I G H T Y I P B
```

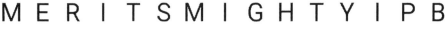

Standing on the Promises

Standing on the promises of **Christ** my **King**,
Through **eternal ages** let His **praises ring**,
Glory in the **highest**, I will **shout** and **sing**,
Standing on the promises of God.

Standing, standing,
Standing on the promises of God my **Savior**;
Standing, standing,
I'm standing on the **promises** of God.

Standing on the promises that cannot **fail**,
When the **howling storms** of **doubt** and **fear**
assail,
By the **living Word** of God I shall **prevail**,
Standing on the promises of God.

Standing on the promises I now can see
Perfect, **present cleansing** in the **blood** for me;
Standing in the **liberty** where Christ makes **free**,
Standing on the promises of God.

Jesus Loves Me

Jesus loves me! This I **know**,
For the **Bible** tells me so;
Little **ones** to Him **belong**;
They are **weak**, but He is **strong**.

Yes, **Jesus** loves me!
Yes, Jesus **loves** me!
Yes, Jesus loves me!
The Bible tells me so.

Jesus loves me! This I know,
As He loved so **long** ago,
Taking **children** on His **knee**,
Saying, "Let them come to Me."

Jesus loves me still **today**,
Walking with me on my way,
Wanting as a **friend** to **give**
Light and love to all who **live**.

```
X J M X R X G W B I M W L V G
Q G T N W N M A G P V B L G G
R C T E I H I N W E L E Y G Z
K F A K I I D T V D F V U J Z
E K L A U B J I L D J E S U S
Z A U M X W G N L I T T L E L
W I X X K S Q G C R A P Y U H
Z D O Z E P O R G G L O A R A
X J A V Q W F N P N Z S E C J
G N O R T S I L X O A Y E B U
M L F A A Y C I G L Q A N I L
O Y K P A U W G G Y I D K Z V
D R F S H O Y H Q X R O O B A
A D S R N B Y T Q I M T D Q P
Y M Q K F Y G N O L E B R Q S
G V V E C D N E I R F D S Y F
E P V B I B L E G O I O Q Z R
W I T S O N E S V Q S O W K Q
L Q M G C S C H I L D R E N K
J H H X J I Q V J N Z K R S I
```

This Is My Father's World

This is my Father's **world**,
And to my **listening** ears
All **nature sings**, and **round** me **rings**
The **music** of the **spheres**.
This is my Father's world:
I rest me in the **thought**
Of **rocks** and **trees**, of **skies** and **seas**--
His **hand** the **wonders wrought**.

This is my Father's world:
The **birds** their **carols raise**,
The **morning light**, the lily **white**,
Declare their Maker's **praise**.
This is my Father's world:
He **shines** in all that's **fair**;
In the **rustling grass** I hear Him **pass**,
He **speaks** to me **everywhere**.

Nearer, My God, to Thee

Nearer, my God, to thee, nearer to thee!
E'en though it be a **cross** that raiseth me,
still all my **song** shall be,
nearer, my God, to thee;
nearer, my God, to thee, nearer to thee!

Though like the **wanderer**, the sun **gone down**,
darkness be over me, my **rest** a **stone**;
yet in my **dreams** I'd be
nearer, my God, to thee;
nearer, my God, to thee, nearer to thee!

There let the way appear, **steps** unto **heaven**;
all that thou **sendest** me, in **mercy given**;
angels to **beckon** me
nearer, my God, to thee;
nearer, my God, to thee, nearer to thee!

Then, with my **waking thoughts bright** with thy **praise**,
out of my stony **griefs Bethel** I'll **raise**;
so by my **woes** to be
nearer, my God, to **thee**;
nearer, my God, to thee, nearer to thee!

G V H B M E X S D Q A M Z S B
K D A E S Z T D A F L E V A O
U Z Y I A H B L R P I R E G N
K P A Q G V E U K U S C U Z L
L R L U N H E O N M H Y L N B
P Y O A T B G N E G N I K A W
K H W E N B R F S W G K M J K
T N B Z A G W I S S O W M E Q
S T E P S Q E U G R M A B U R
I C X H P V V L E H X C C E A
E D U I Z Q A S S J T Q R R L
C G Z O U X I F T L B E E W D
X I P X W A Q S I E D R N N R
G Z P X R Z E H C N A G W U E
R G O N E R T K A E N T O R A
E T S Q L Z O W N O A W D X M
N U S S E N D E S T C T Q N S
O V O R G M G R I E F S H T B
T M R C P K F T V U G W O E S
S A C O S G I V E N R Y N K E

Trust and obey

When we **walk** with the Lord
in the **light** of his **word**,
what a **glory** he **sheds** on our way!
While we do his **good** will,
he **abides** with us still,
and with all who will **trust** and **obey**.

Trust and obey, for there's no other way
to be **happy** in **Jesus**, but to trust and obey.

Not a **burden** we **bear**,
not a **sorrow** we **share**,
but our **toil** he doth **richly repay**;
not a **grief** or a **loss**,
not a **frown** or a **cross**,
but is **blest** if we trust and obey.

But we **never** can **prove**
the **delights** of his love
until all on the **altar** we lay;
for the **favor** he **shows**,
for the joy he **bestows**,
are for them who will trust and obey.

Take My Life and Let It Be

Take my **life**, and let it be
Consecrated, Lord, to Thee;
Take my **moments** and my **days**,
Let them **flow** in ceaseless **praise**,
Let them flow in **ceaseless** praise.

Take my **hands**, and let them **move**
At the **impulse** of Thy **love**;
Take my **feet** and let them be
Swift and beautiful for Thee,
Swift and **beautiful** for Thee.

Take my **voice**, and let me **sing**
Always, only, for my **King**;
Take my **lips**, and let them be
Filled with **messages** from Thee,
Filled with messages from **Thee**.

Take my **silver** and my **gold**;
Not a mite would I **withhold**;
Take my **intellect**, and use
Every **power** as Thou shalt choose,
Every power as Thou shalt **choose**.

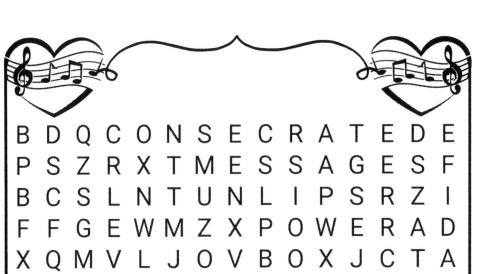

```
B D Q C O N S E C R A T E D E
P S Z R X T M E S S A G E S F
B C S L N T U N L I P S R Z I
F F G E W M Z X P O W E R A D
X Q M V L J O V B O X J C T A
J O H E V E E H V E I C Y Y
M T Z Y F S S Z E T O E V D S
C I D P O I J A Y H L I T F I
C J P O L B L E E L G E C F C
U A H G O L D T E C E S V E W
U C I W V P R T H F Y Y T T W
B G D I E J N E U E P E L F T
C B V T G I P H V A E H R I E
J G X H M H W P C L K N G W R
F X S H G A U O A N I I E S P
I N I O N N Y N L L N S N G R
L M N L A D R D Q F W I Z G A
L A G D R S G I D K Y A Z I I
E L I M P U L S E D Z Y Y S S
D L U F I T U A E B O J G S E
```

O Come, All Ye Faithful

O come, all ye **faithful**, **joyful** and **triumphant**,
O come ye, O come ye to **Bethlehem**!
Come, and **behold** Him, **born** the **King** of **angels**!

O come, let us **adore** Him;
O **come**, let us adore Him;
O come, let us adore Him, **Christ**, the **Lord**!

God of God, **Light** of Light,
lo, He **abhors** not the virgin's **womb**;
very God, **begotten** not **created**;

Sing, **choirs** of angels; sing in **exultation**;
sing, all ye **citizens** of heav'n **above**!
Glory to God, all glory in the **highest**!

Yea, Lord, we **greet** Thee, born this **happy**
morning;
Jesus, to Thee be all glory giv'n!
Word of the **Father**, now in **flesh** **appearing**!

Nothing but the blood

What can **wash** **away** my sin?
Nothing but the blood of Jesus.
What can **make** me **whole again**?
Nothing but the **blood** of Jesus.

O **precious** is the **flow**
that makes me **white** as **snow**;
no other **fount** I **know**;
nothing but the blood of **Jesus**.

For my **pardon** this I see:
nothing but the blood of Jesus.
For my **cleansing** this my **plea**:
nothing but the blood of Jesus.

Nothing can for sin **atone**:
nothing but the blood of Jesus.
Naught of **good** that I have **done**:
nothing but the blood of Jesus.

My Hope Is Built on Nothing Less

My hope is **built** on **nothing less**
than Jesus' **blood** and **righteousness**;
I dare not **trust** the **sweetest frame**,
but **wholly** lean on Jesus' **name**.

On **Christ**, the **solid Rock**, I **stand**:
all other **ground** is sinking **sand**;
all other ground is **sinking** sand.

When **darkness** veils his **lovely** face,
I **rest** on his **unchanging grace**;
in **every high** and **stormy gale**,
my **anchor holds** within the **veil**.

His **oath**, his **covenant**, his blood,
support me in the **whelming flood**;
when all **around** my **soul gives** way,
he then is all my **hope** and **stay**.

Come, Christians, Join to Sing

Come, **Christians**, join to **sing**
Alleluia, Amen!
Loud praise to **Christ** our **King**,
Alleluia, **Amen**!
Let all, with **heart** and **voice**,
before His **throne rejoice**;
praise is His **gracious choice**,
Alleluia, Amen!

Come, **lift** your hearts on **high**,
Alleluia, Amen!
Let praises **fill** the sky,
Alleluia, Amen!
He is our **Guide** and **Friend**,
to us He'll **condescend**;
His **love** shall **never** end,
Alleluia, Amen!

Sweet Hour of Prayer

Sweet hour of prayer! sweet hour of prayer!
That **calls** me from a **world** of **care**,
And **bids** me at my Father's **throne**
Make all my wants and **wishes** **known**.
In **seasons** of **distress** and **grief**,
My **soul** has often **found** **relief**
And oft **escaped** the tempter's **snare**
By thy return, sweet **hour** of **prayer**!

Sweet hour of prayer! sweet hour of prayer!
The **joys** I feel, the **bliss** I **share**,
Of those whose **anxious** **spirits** **burn**
With **strong** **desires** for thy **return**!
With such I **hasten** to the **place**
Where God my **Savior** shows His **face**,
And **gladly** take my **station** there,
And **wait** for thee, sweet hour of prayer!

Praise to the Lord, the Almighty

Praise to the Lord, the **Almighty**, the **King** of **creation**!
O my **soul**, praise him, for he is your **health** and **salvation**!
Come, all who **hear**; now to his **temple** draw near,
join me in **glad adoration**.

Praise to the Lord, **above** all things so **wondrously reigning**;
sheltering you under his **wings**, and so **gently sustaining**!
Have you not seen all that is **needful** has been sent by his **gracious ordaining**?

Praise to the **Lord**, who will **prosper** your **work** and **defend** you;
surely his **goodness** and **mercy** shall **daily attend** you.
Ponder anew what the Almighty can do,
if with his love he **befriends** you.

Abide With Me

Abide with me – fast **falls** the **eventide**,
The **darkness deepens** – Lord, with me abide;
When other **helpers** fail and **comforts** flee,
Help of the helpless, O abide with me!

Swift to its **close** ebbs out life's **little** day;
Earth's joys grow dim, its **glories** pass away;
Change and **decay** in all **around** I see –
O Thou who changest not, abide with me!

I need Thy **presence** ev'ry **passing hour** –
What but Thy **grace** can foil the tempter's pow'r?
Who, like Thyself, my **guide** and stay can be?
Thru **cloud** and **sunshine**, O abide with me.

I fear no foe, with Thee at **hand** to **bless**;
Ills have no **weight**, and **tears** no **bitterness**.
Where is death's **sting**? Where, **grave**, thy
victory?
I **triumph** still, if Thou abide with me.

F N Y H E D E F A L L S X V H
Y Z O D V E A H X T L H P R A
I U I F O Z W R R M T E J E D
R U C L O U D I K B E N L A E
G G B M Z K U G V N V I S R C
O R D J R M S Y Q N E H H O A
Q A N W P B T R X O N S S U Y
S V Y H B B I O I S T N S N E
E E D E E X N T U Y I U W D C
C U Z L G C G C T H D S W M A
N G C I N I Q I P E E D T Z R
E N T T A F L V W B R E X B G
S I F T H V E E L R A N N S O
E S I L C D I E I R K E E B Y
R S W E I G S R S O D H I S I
P A S B H S O P I A T M N C S
Y P A T S R E P L E H V I U G
D E E P E N S H D H E S O L C
A A T R U C O M F O R T S G D
P T G L O R I E S H A N D I O

All Creatures of Our God

All **creatures** of our God and **King**,
lift up your voice and with us **sing**,
"**Alleluia**! Alleluia!"
Thou **burning** sun with **golden beam**,
thou **silver moon** with **softer gleam**,
O **praise** Him, O praise Him!
alleluia, alleluia, alleluia!

Thou **rushing wind** that art so **strong**,
ye **clouds** that sail in heav'n **along**,
O praise Him! Alleluia!
Thou **rising** morn, in praise **rejoice**,
ye **lights** of ev'ning, find a **voice**,
O praise Him, O praise Him!
alleluia, alleluia, alleluia!

And all ye men of **tender heart**,
forgiving others, take your **part**,
O sing ye! Alleluia!
Ye who **long pain** and **sorrow bear**,
praise God and on Him cast your **care**;
O praise Him, O praise Him!
alleluia, alleluia, alleluia!

Amazing grace

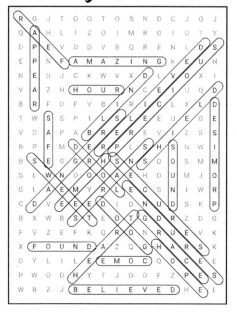

How great thou art

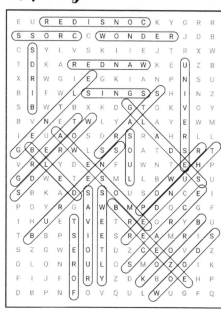

Great Is Thy Faithfulness

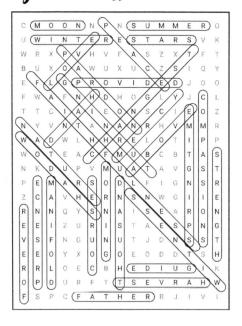

Holy, Holy, Holy

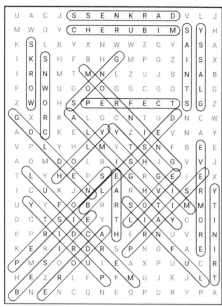

Be Thou My Vision

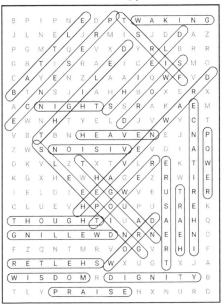

It Is Well with My Soul

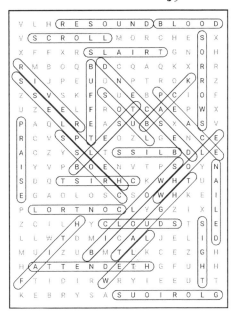

Blessed Assurance

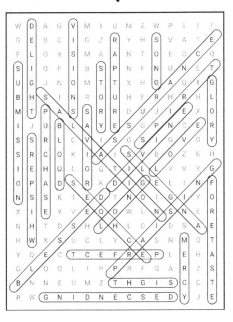

The Old Rugged Cross

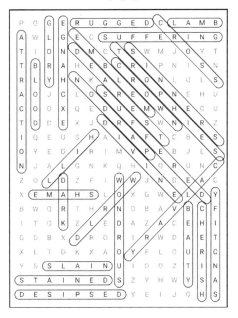

A Mighty Fortress

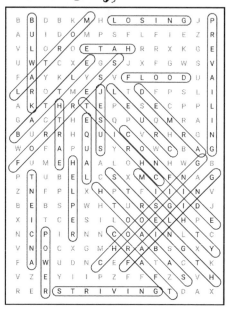

Come Thou Fount

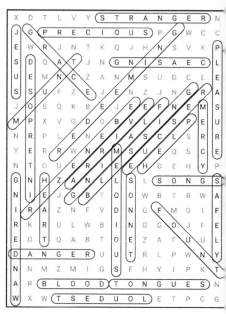

What a Friend We Have

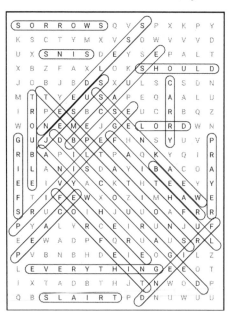

Jesus Paid It All

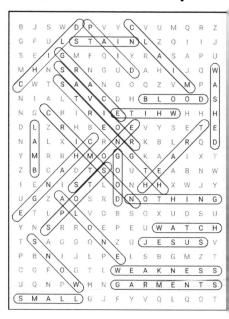

To God Be the Glory

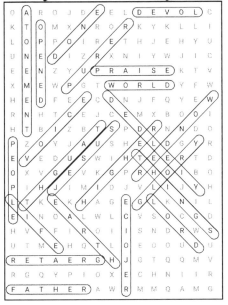

Rock of Ages

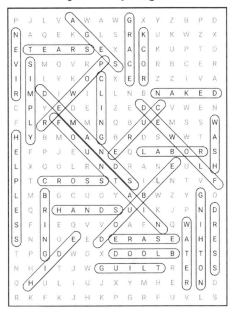

Just As I Am

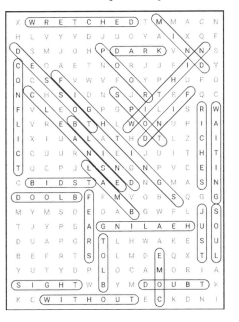

Crown Him with Many Crowns

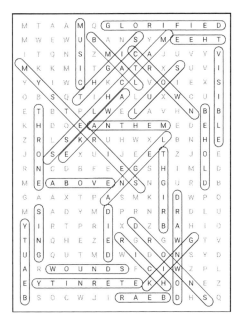

All Hail the Power

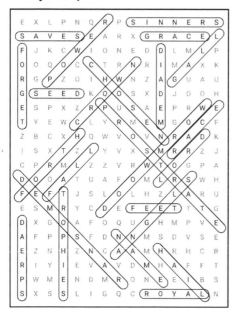

Fairest Lord Jesus

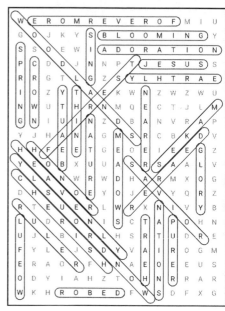

I Surrender All

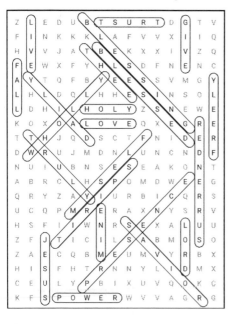

O for a Thousand Tongues

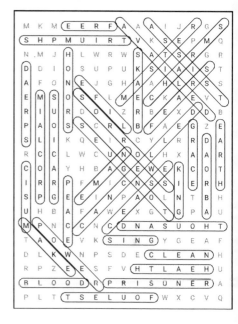

Joyful, Joyful, We Adore Thee

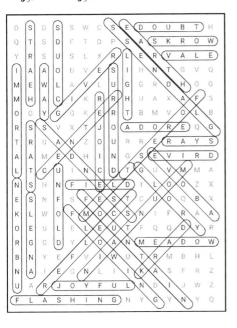

I Need Thee Every Hour

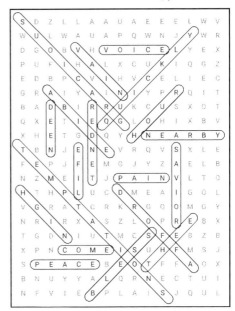

Because He Lives

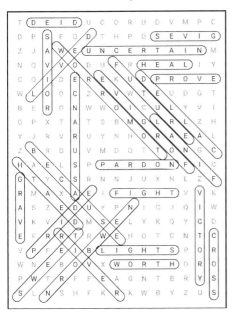

When I Survey

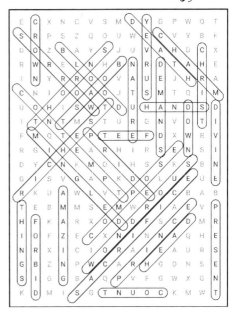

Turn Your Eyes Upon Jesus

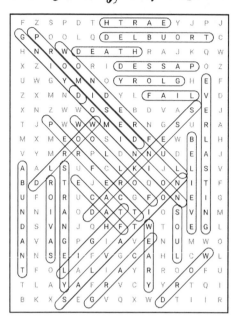

Christ the Lord Is Risen Today

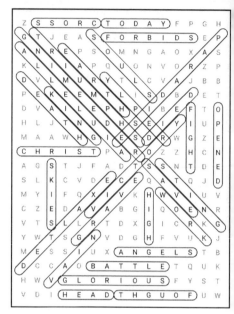

He Lives

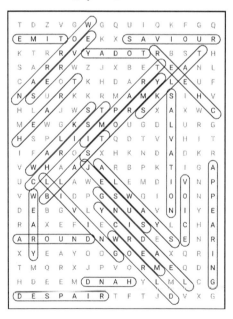

I'd Rather Have Jesus

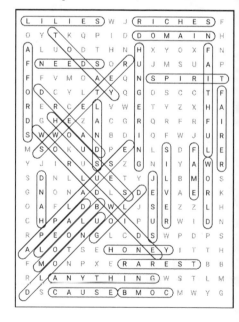

Victory in Jesus

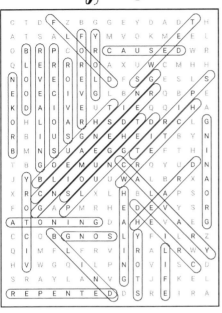

Love Lifted Me

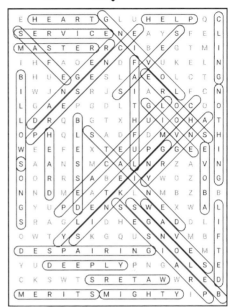

Standing on the Promises

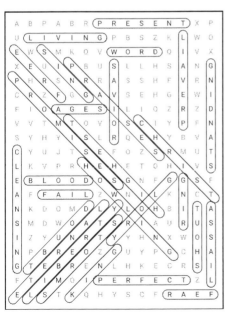

Jesus Loves Me

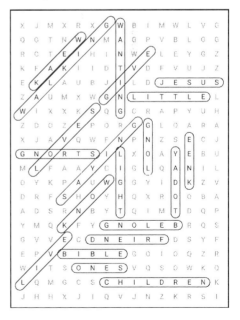

This Is My Father's World

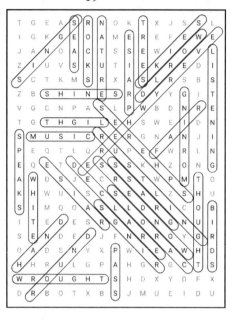

Nearer, My God, to Thee

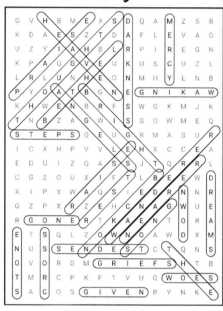

Trust and obey

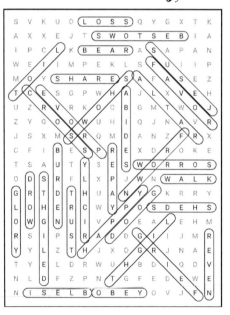

Take My Life and Let It Be

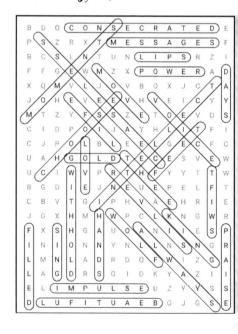

O Come, All Ye Faithful

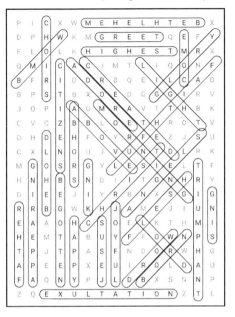

Nothing but the blood

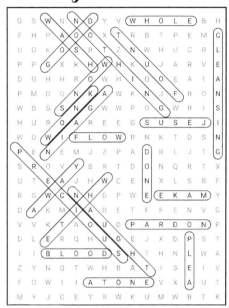

My Hope Is Built

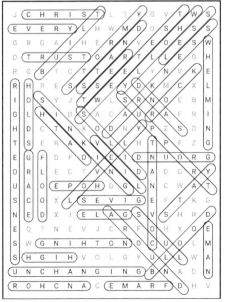

Come, Christians

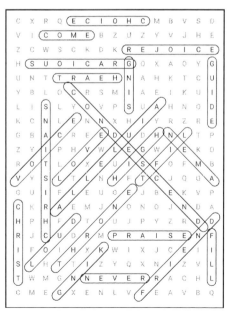

Sweet Hour of Prayer

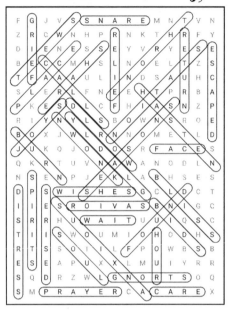

Praise to the Lord, the Almighty

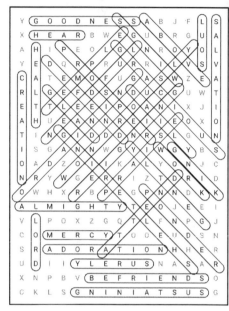

Abide With Me

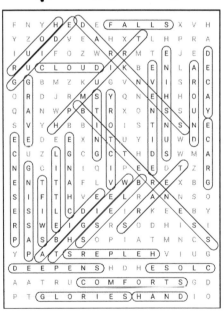

All Creatures of Our God

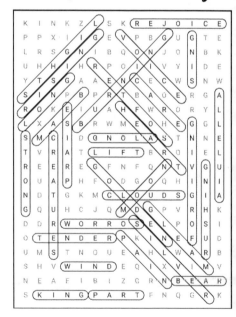

Thank You For Your Support!

We hope you enjoyed our book!
Your feedback is valuable to us. If you
have a moment, please consider
leaving a review. Your thoughts help
us improve and create even better
puzzles for you. Thank you!

Made in United States
Orlando, FL
05 December 2024

55043753R00057